MAR 2005

Night Shift Daddy

Eileen Spinelli

Illustrated by
Melissa Iwai

Hyperion Books for Children/New York

For information address Hyperion Books for Children,
114 Fifth Avenue, New York, New York 10011-5690.

Visit www.hyperionchildrensbooks.com

Printed in Hong Kong

FIRST EDITION
7 9 10 8

This book is set in Guardi Roman.

Library of Congress Cataloging-in-Publication Data
Spinelli, Eileen.
Night Shift Daddy/Eileen Spinelli; illustrated by Melissa Iwai—1st ed.
p.   cm.
Summary: A father shares dinner and bedtime rituals with his daughter
before going out to work the night shift.
ISBN 0-7868-0495-5 (hardcover)—ISBN 0-7868-2424-7 (library)
[1. Fathers and daughters—Fiction. 2. Bedtime—Fiction.
3. Stories in rhyme.] I. Iwai, Melissa, ill. II. Title.
PZ8.3.S759Ni   2000
[E]—dc21   98-52499

ight shift Daddy swings me high,
shares his milk and apple pie,

rocks me in the rocking chair,
reads to me and Teddy Bear.

Soon the winter sun goes down,
shadows spill across the town.

Daddy says it's time for bed,
calls me little sleepyhead,
fluffs my pillow, tucks me in—
pulls covers up around my chin.

He kisses me and tweaks my nose.
He says: "How cozy are those toes?"

And then, "Sweet dreams!"
And then, "Good night."
And then he switches
off the light.

He doesn't know I watch him go
into the cold, the dark, the snow—

down to the bus stop, bundled up,
holding his thermal coffee cup.

I watch him as our house clocks chime.
His bus comes rolling right on time.

He's off to work—
I'm off to sleep and off to dream.

He's off to sweep.

The moon grows pale behind a tree.

The morning sun awakens me.

Night shift Daddy's home by eight
to share a pancake from my plate.

I lead him to the rocking chair,
then read to him and Teddy Bear.

Soon night shift Daddy nods his head.
I say I think it's time for bed.
I fluff his pillow, tuck him in—
pull covers up around his chin.

I kiss him hard and tweak his nose.
I say: "How cozy are those toes?"

And then, "Sweet dreams!"
And then, "Sleep tight."

I close the curtains to the light.

While night shift Daddy snores away

I dress myself, go out and play.